ASK

ASK OSCAR

ALAN MACDONALD

ILLUSTRATED BY SARAH HORNE

EGMONT

For Lewis, Bridie and Laurie and all the pets that lived with us.
AM

For the children at COHAD. Kumi, Uganda
SH

EGMONT

We bring stories to life

First published in Great Britain in 2018
by Egmont UK Limited
The Yellow Building, 1 Nicholas Road, London W11 4AN

The moral rights of the author and cover illustrator have been asserted

ISBN 978 1 4052 8722 7

www.egmont.co.uk

A CIP catalogue record for this title is available from the British Library
Typeset by Avon DataSet Ltd, Bidford on Avon, Warwickshire
Printed and bound in Great Britain by the CPI Group

67270/1

MIX
Paper from
responsible sources
FSC® C020471

CONTENTS

Chapter 1

Dog on the Bus

The dog was on the number 9 bus. Buses went past Sam's house every day but normally they didn't have a dog on the top deck. He was sitting all by himself as if he had a ticket and travelled by bus all the time. As the bus flashed past Sam's bedroom window, the dog turned his head and looked straight at him. The expression on his face seemed to say, 'Well look at that – a boy in his bedroom wearing only one sock!' (Sam was in the middle of dressing at the time as he'd just come out of the bath.)

1

In seconds the bus was gone and Sam was left
wondering if he'd imagined the whole thing.
Perhaps he hadn't noticed the dog's owner
bending down or hiding on the floor? Perhaps
it wasn't a dog at all but a man with a hairy
beard and whiskers wearing a fur coat? Were
dogs even allowed on buses? Sam didn't know.
Maybe the truth was that he just had dogs on

the brain because he'd been asking his parents to let him have one for ages. In fact, asking was an understatement. He'd been begging, nagging and pleading – and when that failed, wishing and praying for a dog.

Over months he'd built up a collection of things a dog might need such as rubber bones, old tennis balls and dog biscuits. He'd tried dropping hints, by mentioning friends who had dogs and hadn't died or caught fleas as a result. He'd even written 'DOG' in capital letters at the top of his birthday list. Yet whatever he said or did made no difference – his parents' answer was the same. A dog just wasn't *'practical'* right now, they said. Dogs were too costly, too messy, too much work – in fact just too 'doggy' altogether.

Downstairs, Sam found the table set for

supper and his mum and dad arguing about something. It seemed to be to do with a pile of bills that had been hidden in the tea caddy. Sam's parents often argued about money, but today he wasn't really listening because he was thinking about the dog on the bus.

'Telephone, gas, water . . .' Mum was saying. 'Have we paid *any* of these?'

Dad waved his fork. 'I was getting round to it,' he said.

'Really? *When?*' demanded Mum.

'When we had a bit more money,' said Dad. 'You know, once business picks up.'

Sam looked at his Mum. Dad said this a lot but business never actually picked up. Mr Shilling worked from home as a self-employed inventor, although he didn't actually earn any money. His latest project, the Grandem – a four-person bike for the whole family – sat out in the shed with all his other unsold inventions. Sam could tell his dad was in trouble but fortunately he was saved by a knock on the door. Actually it wasn't a knock, it was more like a muffled thump.

'Oh, who's that?' asked Dad.

'No idea,' said Mum. 'But we haven't finished talking.'

'Maybe it's the postman?' suggested Sam.

'Not on a Sunday evening,' said Dad.

The thump came again two or three times, followed by a sound like scrabbling or scratching. If it was the postman he was behaving very oddly.

'I'll go!' said Sam, curious to see who it was.

But when he opened the door there was no one there. He was about to close it when he looked down – and noticed the black and white dog on the doorstep gazing up at him expectantly. It had a thick, wiry coat, dark eyes and an intelligent face. Its tail was wagging like a windscreen wiper. Sam's heart leapt. It was the kind of dog he'd always dreamed of owning and what's more he'd seen it before, on the top deck of the bus.

'Who is it?' Mum called from the kitchen.

'Nobody!' Sam shouted back.

His mind raced. If he said there was a strange dog at the door he knew his parents would come and shoo it away. But he didn't want the dog to go yet – it had only just arrived and it had come all this way on the bus! He crouched down, stroking the dog's shaggy coat. It nuzzled up to him readily and gave his face a lick. Sam laughed.

'Shh!' he said. 'Don't make a noise!'

The dog blinked. It stopped washing his face, then pushed past him into the hall.

It looked around as if deciding whether the house was up to scratch.

'Sam, what are you doing?'

It was his Mum again and she sounded impatient.

'Nothing. Just coming!' Sam called back.

He'd have to move fast. There was nothing for it but to hide the dog, at least until he'd worked out what to do with him. The shed was no good because Dad used it as his workshop. The only safe place was Sam's bedroom but that meant smuggling the dog through the house and upstairs without his parents seeing him.

Sam noticed the dog had a leather collar with a silver name disc. It said, 'OSCAR'.

'Go round to the back door, Oscar,' Sam whispered, leading him out again. 'I'll let you in, but no barking, okay?'

He realised it was asking a lot for the dog to understand – he might as well be speaking Norwegian – but amazingly the dog obeyed. He went out and trotted round the side of the house as if he knew the way. Sam quickly shut the front door and headed back to the kitchen, trying to look as if nothing unusual had happened, like a dog appearing from nowhere.

'What took you so long?' demanded his Mum.

'I was just checking there wasn't anyone there,' explained Sam. 'It must have been the wind.'

'It didn't sound like the wind,' said Dad. 'I swear I heard scratching.'

'Maybe it was Mr Trusscot next door?' suggested Sam. 'He scratches sometimes.'

'Not so loudly that you can hear him through the walls,' said Mum.

Mr Trusscot was their annoying neighbour who was also Leader of the Town Council, as he often reminded them. Sam had been slowly edging out of the kitchen. He needed to get to the back door in case the dog started whining and gave them away.

'Where are you off to now?' asked Mum.

'Um, I've got homework,' said Sam.

'But you haven't even finished your supper,' argued Mum.

'It's a lot of homework,' said Sam, ducking out of the door. He hurried down the hall. Luckily his parents soon went back to their argument about the bills.

Oscar was waiting outside the back door. He immediately padded in, wagging his tail so hard that it practically dented the doorframe. Somehow Sam had to get him through the hall, past the kitchen and up the stairs without making any noise. He decided he'd better communicate with the dog by mime, acting out what he had in mind. Pointing upwards, he pretended to be climbing some stairs on tiptoe. Oscar watched patiently with his head on one side as if this was a new sort of game – like doggy charades.

Sam set off down the hall with the dog padding at his heels. The kitchen door was half open and his parents were still talking. With a bit of luck he might be able to sneak Oscar past without them seeing anything. Sam ducked his head and went first . . .

'SAM!'

He froze in the doorway, trying to block his parents' view of the hall.

'Yes?' he said, his heart racing. If he looked down he was afraid he'd see Oscar's whiskery face peering out between his legs.

'Don't forget to pack your school bag for the

morning,' said Mum. 'Are you *all right?*'

'Me? Yes! Fine, I'll do it later,' promised Sam.

He backed out quickly and closed the kitchen door. That was close. But looking round, his heart missed a beat. The dog had disappeared! Where had he got to *now*? If he'd slipped past Sam into the kitchen then the game was up. Sam rushed down the hall. He checked the lounge and the downstairs toilet. No dog. The front door was closed so he couldn't have got out. Turning round, he caught sight of something. Oscar sat at the top of the stairs, waiting patiently. He cocked his head on one side as if to say, 'Really, that wasn't so difficult, was it?'

All that evening Sam stayed in his room on the pretence that he was getting on with his homework. Actually he spent the time introducing Oscar to his collection of doggy toys. Later, Sam crept downstairs and managed to sneak a bowl of water from the kitchen. Naturally he knew that they couldn't go on like this forever. Eventually Oscar would be discovered or Sam would have to tell his parents, but he didn't want to think about that. For the moment he had a dog of his own and he wanted to make it last as long as possible.

Later, when he heard his mum coming upstairs, he hid Oscar under the bed. Turning off the main light he dived back under the covers just as his mum's head appeared round the door.

'Night, night, love, sleep tight!' she said, softly.

'Night,' mumbled Sam, praying that the dog wouldn't make a sound.

The door clicked shut. Sam crept out from under this duvet and opened his cupboard. He found an old beanbag for Oscar to sleep on – at least that was the idea. Some hours later when the house was dark and his parents were in bed, he heard the soft patter of feet. A second later, Oscar leapt up onto the bed and licked his nose.

'Hello!' Sam laughed.

Eventually they settled down to sleep with Oscar making himself comfortable on top of the duvet. Sam rolled onto his side and closed his eyes.

'Good night, Oscar,' he murmured drowsily.

'Night.'

Sam's eyes flew open. He switched on his

bedside lamp and sat up, looking around wildly. There was no one else in the room, only the dog dozing peacefully on the duvet.

'Ridiculous, I must have been dreaming,' Sam told himself. 'Dogs definitely *cannot* talk.'

Chapter 2

Hide and Sneak

The next day was Monday, a school day, which posed an awkward problem – what to do with Oscar? Sam considered taking him to school but he was pretty sure dogs weren't allowed. Even if he dressed Oscar in a shirt and school tie he didn't think Miss Bramble would be fooled. He'd have to hide him at home somewhere his parents weren't likely to look. But where? A dog under the duvet would look pretty obvious and anyway Oscar wouldn't stay there for long.

Sam looked around, trying to think. Of course – the clothes cupboard! Sam's bedroom had a large built-in cupboard with shelves piled high with clothes, books, comics and toys. If he cleared some space on the floor there was plenty of room for a not-too-large dog. He dragged the beanbag into the cupboard.

'In you go, boy,' he said, pointing. Oscar looked at the cupboard then back at him. He didn't budge.

'Come on, Oscar, it's not for long, just while I'm at school,' pleaded Sam. 'Once Mum and Dad know, you won't have to hide.'

In the end, Sam had to pick Oscar up and carry him into the cupboard. He left him with a supply of dog biscuits, a bowl of water and the rubber bone to play with in case he got bored. It wasn't ideal, he told himself, but it was only for today. As long as Dad didn't go nosing in his room then Oscar would be safe – and it would give him time to break the news that they were

getting a dog.

All that day at school, Sam's thoughts kept returning to Oscar. He worried that he might be scared of the dark. What if he started barking or whining and his dad went up to investigate? (His mum worked part time as a physio at the hospital so she wasn't at home on Mondays). Sam was dying to tell someone, so eventually he let his best friend, Louie, in on the secret half way through maths.

'A DOG?' cried Louie.

'Shh! Keep your voice down!' whispered Sam. 'It's a secret!' He glanced up. Miss Bramble was busy helping someone with their work.

'But where did you get him?' asked Louie.

Sam briefly explained how Oscar had arrived on the bus.

'That's fantastic!' enthused Louie. 'We could take him for walks – we could go to the beach!'

'If he stays,' said Sam. 'My parents don't even know about him yet. I had to hide him in my cupboard.'

Louie's eyebrows shot up. 'You've left him in a cupboard?'

'It's quite a big one and he's got biscuits,' explained Sam. 'But if my parents find him they'll go mad.'

'You're the one that's mad,' said Louie.

But they didn't get any further because Miss Bramble told them off for talking instead of getting on with their work.

As soon as the bell went, Sam grabbed his bag and ran all the way home. He'd been plagued by worries all day. What if Dad had discovered Oscar and thrown him out? They hadn't even had the chance to get to know each other!

Arriving home, Sam dumped his bag and ran upstairs. He found his Dad hoovering the landing.

'Ah, Sam, perfect timing,' he said, switching the machine off. 'I was just about to do your room.'

His room? Sam looked aghast.

'You can't!' he said. 'I mean, my pyjamas are all over the floor. I haven't tidied up!'

'Well you can tidy it now,' said Dad. 'But get a move on, I haven't got all day.'

Sam dashed into his bedroom and closed the door. He was surprised to see the cupboard door was wide open. Somehow Oscar had managed to get out because he was curled on the bed with a book open. (It was a picture book about pirates and for a moment Sam imagined he was reading it). In the cupboard were a scattering of biscuit crumbs and a damp patch on the carpet that might have been water but probably wasn't. Oscar yawned, rolled onto his side and stretched out lazily.

Sam had to think fast. He could put Oscar back in the cupboard but what if his Dad tried to tidy something away when he was hoovering the room? The only other solution was to smuggle Oscar out of the house. But how could he get past his dad on the landing? Suddenly he saw a possible way out – the laundry basket! Sam reckoned it was probably just big enough to hold Oscar if he made himself small.

A few moments later Sam emerged from his room, dragging the laundry basket with an effort. Oscar was a lot heavier than he'd expected and he was hidden under a pile of dirty T-shirts, socks and pants.

'Finally!' said Dad. 'What's that?'

'My dirty washing,' said Sam. 'I thought I'd take it down to the washing machine for er . . . washing.'

'Right,' said Dad, sounding puzzled. Generally Sam regarded washing and ironing as something that happened as if by magic.

Sam staggered forward and Dad stepped aside to let him past. He could feel his dad's eyes on him as he reached the stairs. The laundry basket was so heavy he was sweating and could hardly get it off the floor. He wished Oscar had been a pug dog or something smaller.

'What on earth have you got in there?' asked Dad.

'Just my clothes and stuff,' said Sam, breathing hard. If he could just make it downstairs then they'd be safe. He heaved the basket after him, setting it down on the next step with a thump. A loud grunt came from inside.

'What was that?' asked Dad.

'What?'

'That noise!'

'It was me,' said Sam. He coughed loudly but Dad wasn't buying it.

'Let me see the basket,' he demanded.

Sam turned round slowly in time to see his dad's eyes grow wide with astonishment. Looking down, Sam saw a pair of blue pants rising up out of the basket. Underneath was a whiskery face and a wet black nose. Oscar sneezed and the pants fell off.

Unluckily at that very moment the front door slammed and Mum came in.

'A DOG!' she screamed.

'Oh yes, so it is,' said Sam, sounding surprised.

'But where . . . how on earth did it get here?' asked Mum.

'On the bus I think,' replied Sam, truthfully.

Mum looked up at Dad. 'Did you know about this?'

'ME?' protested Dad. 'It's nothing to do with me!'

Mum folded her arms. 'Right, get down here, Sam and bring the dog,' she said. 'We need to have a serious talk.'

Chapter 3

The One and Only

Sam's parents weren't happy at all to discover he'd been hiding a dog in his bedroom since yesterday evening. They said he should have told them the moment the dog had arrived. Sam tried to explain that he was fully *intending* to tell them, he was just waiting for the right moment, but it didn't help. Mum said that if they adopted every stray mutt that came to the door they'd soon be running a dog's home, which Sam thought sounded a pretty good idea. In any case Dad pointed out that Oscar probably had an owner who was looking for him right now. Sam hadn't really considered this. All he knew was that Oscar had come to *him* – surely that counted for something?

In the end, Sam was allowed to take Oscar for a walk while his parents discussed what to do. Sam decided to call for Louie on the way to the beach because he knew he'd understand. Besides, he wanted to show him Oscar while he still had the chance.

The beach at Little Bunting wasn't the kind to attract crowds of holidaymakers. It was mostly shingle with a stretch of sand and a few rock pools at low tide. This made it popular with joggers and dog walkers. Today however, the beach was deserted, leaving acres of space for Oscar to run around. He scampered off, poking his nose into green pools and chasing seagulls, which flapped away before he got close.

'This is great,' said Louie. 'Our very own dog!'

'Ours?' said Sam.

'Well okay, yours,' admitted Louie. 'But we can share him, can't we? I mean, I don't mind taking him for walks.'

Sam wasn't sure he was ready to share Oscar, not yet anyway.

'Maybe you'll get your own dog,' he suggested.

'Fat chance,' said Louie. 'I told you my sister's got rabbits and we're not allowed any more pets.'

'Well, my parents are no different,' said Sam. 'They've never wanted a dog.'

'But I bet they'll change their minds,' said Louie.

Sam shook his head, sadly. 'Dad thinks

they're a lot of trouble and Mum doesn't really like dogs.'

'How can you *not* like *dogs?*' asked Louie, shaking his head at the endless weirdness of parents. He tried to make a stone skim across the waves but it vanished with a plop.

'Why don't we teach him some tricks?' he suggested. 'You can show your mum and dad how clever he is.'

Sam wasn't convinced this would help. Oscar *was* clever, but he was still a dog with doggy smells and habits. Right now he was sticking his nose into a pile of pongy seaweed.

'Hey Oscar, let's play a game,' said Louie, squatting down.

Oscar came trotting over with his tongue hanging out.

'We'll start with something easy,' said Louie.

'Let's teach him to sit. The trick with dogs is to let them know you're in charge.'

Sam raised his eyebrows. For someone who'd never actually owned a dog, Louie seemed to know a lot about it.

'OSCAR, SIT!' commanded Louie, sternly.

'SIT! SIT, BOY! SIT!

'*OSCAR, SIT!*'

This produced no response at all. Oscar remained on four legs, glancing up at a passing seagull.

'Let me have a go,' suggested Sam. 'Hey Oscar, let's sit down, shall we?'

He sat down on the shingle to demonstrate.

'That's no use!' scoffed Louie. 'He doesn't understand.'

But Oscar suddenly sat down, and then lay down.

Sam grinned. 'You were saying?'

'Well it's a start I suppose,' admitted Louie, grudgingly. 'But he's going to need a lot more training. Why don't I fetch my Frisbee and we'll see if he can catch? Wait there, I'll be back in a minute!'

Louie set off, scrambling up the beach, losing his footing then springing up again to reach the steps. Sam watched him go. He picked up a stick and sat down beside Oscar. For a moment or two they watched the waves roll in.

'I'm not an idiot, you know.'

Sam shot to his feet as if he'd just sat on a red ants' nest. He stared at Oscar and then

looked around wildly to see who else on the beach could have spoken. There was no one to be seen for miles.

'What . . . what did you say?' stammered Sam, peering closer.

'I said, "I'm not an idiot",' replied Oscar. 'Any fool can sit. Even cats can do it.'

His mouth moved and *words actually came out*. Sam didn't know whether to laugh or scream or pinch himself to see if he was awake.

'You can TALK!' he cried.

'Don't look so surprised,' said Oscar.

'But you're a dog – I mean, dogs can't talk,' objected Sam.

'I believe I'm talking to you now,' said Oscar. 'Besides, dogs talk to each other all the time. It's just that you can't tell what we're saying.'

Sam felt a need to sit down before he fell

over. He couldn't believe he was having a conversation with a dog. Then he remembered the voice he'd heard last night wishing him goodnight. He hadn't imagined it after all! His head was bursting with so many questions that he hardly knew where to start.

'Are there other dogs like you?' he asked. 'I mean dogs that can talk like people?'

Oscar thought. 'I've never met one,' he said. 'I like to think I'm the one and only me.'

'But where did you learn?' asked Sam.

'I didn't learn, it just comes naturally,' said Oscar. 'Like digging holes or chasing squirrels.'

Sam tried to take this in. It opened up a whole new world of possibilities – things he'd always wondered about but could never ask.

'What's it like?' he asked. 'Being a dog?'

Oscar blinked at him. 'Much better than

being a boy,' he said.

'Oh well, I don't know about that,' laughed Sam.

'I do. Dogs are superior in every way,' declared Oscar. 'Take legs for instance. How many do you have?'

'Well, two,' replied Sam, looking down.

'Precisely. Dogs have four which is exactly the right number,' Oscar explained. 'We can run faster and we don't fall over like your friend just now. What about your tail?'

Sam blinked. 'I don't have one.'

'I do and it's extremely useful,' said Oscar. 'How can you show you're pleased without wagging your tail? No, humans are all right in their way but they're nothing like dogs. No tail, no sense of smell – if you ask me they need a great deal of training.'

Sam blinked. He'd never thought of the world in this light. He'd always loved dogs but he'd assumed that they were ... well, just dogs – excitable, loyal, obedient, but not half as clever as people. Oscar seemed to be suggesting that dogs were the real masters and people were the pets – nice but a bit clueless.

'While we're here let's set out a few ground rules,' said Oscar. 'First of all, I'm not sleeping in a cupboard. I'm not a pair of trousers, you know.'

Sam pulled a face. 'Sorry, I didn't know where else to hide you,' he said.

'Well it's too late for hiding,' said Oscar. 'And I don't fetch sticks, just in case you were thinking of throwing that one.'

Sam remembered the stick in his hand and dropped it quickly.

'I thought dogs *liked* fetching sticks?' he said.

'Some dogs do,' agreed Oscar. 'But I've never seen the point myself. I mean – throw – run – fetch, throw – run – fetch and so on and so on. If you want the stick, why do you keep throwing it?'

Sam shrugged. 'It's a game.'

'You're not the one doing all the fetching,' said Oscar. 'And one other thing – dog food.'

'Yes, sorry, we've only got biscuits at the moment,' said Sam.

'Just as well!' said Oscar. 'Most dog food is disgusting – smelly, lumpy, gloopy stuff. Have you ever actually *tried* it?'

'Well no, it's meant for dogs,' said Sam.

'Not *this* dog,' said Oscar. 'I don't want to sound fussy but if your parents mention dog food, try suggesting something else like chicken livers.'

Sam nodded. Oscar seemed very particular. Most dogs he knew would eat anything, even if it came from a dustbin. In any case, Oscar was talking as if he was staying but at the moment that was far from certain. A new thought suddenly occurred to him.

'How are we going to tell them?' he asked.

'Who?'

'My mum and dad. They'll die of shock when they discover you can talk.'

Oscar raised his ears. 'Which is exactly why we *won't* tell them,' he said.

'But aren't they bound to find out?' asked Sam.

'I don't see why,' said Oscar. 'As far as they're concerned I'm just a dog, a clever one of course, but still a dog. I won't talk when they're around and if you speak to me I shall simply bark or whine.'

'You mean it has to be a secret?' said Sam.

'Exactly,' agreed Oscar. 'Your parents would only make an almighty fuss if they found out. Eventually they'd tell someone else and that someone would tell a few others and in no time half the world would know. I wouldn't be able to cross the street without people wanting to hear me talk or sing or recite a poem.'

'Oh,' said Sam. 'I hadn't thought of that.'

'No, if you want me to stay it's much better we keep it a secret,' said Oscar.

'Are you *going* to stay?' asked Sam, hopefully.

'If you're lucky and it all goes smoothly,' replied Oscar. 'But it's your parents who'll make the decision. The trick is to help them get it right.'

'How do we do that?' asked Sam.

'Well, that's what we have to work on,' said Oscar. 'But don't look so worried, I think they're warming to me already.'

Sam wished he shared the same confidence. So far Oscar had weed in the bedroom cupboard and given Dad the fright of his life. It wasn't the best of starts.

'Ah look, here comes your funny friend,' said Oscar. 'I'd better play dumb. Not a word, remember.'

Louie came running down the beach towards them, waving a red plastic Frisbee. Sam glanced at Oscar. He wondered how on earth he was going to keep this a secret. What if his mum or dad overheard the two of them talking one day? And there was Louie too; they'd been best friends since the first week of school. It wasn't going to be easy hiding it from him. Then again, Louie was pretty hopeless at keeping secrets. He had a habit of blurting things out when he got overexcited, which was quite a lot.

'Hey Oscar, what's this, boy?' he cried,

waving the Frisbee under the dog's nose.

He drew back his arm and sent it spinning away into the sky.

'FETCH, OSCAR!' he cried. 'FETCH, BOY! FETCH!'

Chapter 4

Sausage Dog

Back home, Mum and Dad were waiting in the kitchen. It was obvious they'd been discussing Oscar because they suddenly fell silent when Sam appeared. Oscar padded over and lay down on the rug like any ordinary dog. Sam, on the other hand, found it difficult to keep still and had to concentrate to keep a grin off his face. But Mum soon changed that.

'Listen Sam, I know you've got your hopes up,' she said. 'But the fact is we just can't keep him.'

Sam's face fell. 'Why not? He's got nowhere

to go!'

'He's wearing a collar, so he must have an owner,' said Dad.

'But what if he hasn't?' argued Sam. '*Then* can we keep him?'

'You know what we've said about dogs,' sighed Mum. 'It's just not practical right now. I go out to work and your dad's busy all day. Besides, there are all the other arguments.'

Sam sighed deeply. They'd been over this a hundred times, so often that he knew his parents' arguments by heart. He knelt down beside Oscar, putting an arm around him.

'You can't just throw him out. It's cruel!' he pleaded.

Oscar sunk his chin on the floor, doing his best 'sad dog' impression.

Mum groaned. 'We're not throwing him out,'

she said. 'We'll phone the police and find out if anyone's reported a lost dog.'

'But meanwhile can't we keep him?' begged Sam.

Mum and Dad exchanged looks.

'Well, just for now,' sighed Dad.

'Thank you!' cried Sam.

Oscar did a little dance around the kitchen. Actually he didn't, but Sam could tell that he wanted to.

At least they'd gained some time, which was a start, thought Sam. Now all they had to do was convince his parents to let Oscar stay. Sam wondered if they'd think differently if they knew Oscar could talk – but he'd promised to keep it a secret so he'd just have to tackle their objections to dogs. Up in his bedroom he explained these to Oscar. They could be summed up briefly in three words: 'messy', 'expensive' and 'hard work' (actually, that was four words).

'Messy?' said Oscar huffily. 'Who are they calling messy?'

'Don't blame me,' said Sam. 'It's just what they think.'

'And how can I be expensive? I think you'll find humans cost far more than dogs,' said Oscar.

'You don't have to tell me,' agreed Sam. After all, dogs didn't need school uniform, football boots or bikes. They didn't go to the hairdressers or paint their nails pink. All a dog really needed was daily walks, food and plenty of affection.

'Maybe it's the food,' suggested Sam. 'I

suppose dog food does cost money.'

'I told you dog food is disgusting gloop,' said Oscar.

'Okay, then we just have to show that feeding you won't cost much,' said Sam. 'You can eat whatever's in the house.'

'I'm not eating vegetables,' warned Oscar. 'I ate a brussell sprout once and I was sick!'

'Come on then,' said Sam. 'Let's find something that you *do* like.'

Downstairs, Sam opened the fridge and began spreading all the food out on the kitchen table. There were eggs, butter, yoghurts, cheese, some cold lasagne, a pot of jam, some leftover baked beans, a bag of salad and half a packet of sausages that had been lurking in the bottom of the fridge. Obviously, Sam knew Oscar wouldn't like *everything* but there ought to be enough to feed him.

'So which of these do you like?' asked Sam.

'I don't know, I'd have to taste them first,' replied Oscar.

'Okay,' said Sam. 'But just a little taste.'

Oscar jumped onto a chair and from there climbed onto the table. He sniffed the jam, sticking his nose into the jar.

'Hmm, no thanks,' he said, pulling a face.

He went on to try the cold lasagne and sample everything on the table in turn. He had just reached the sausages, which received a thorough licking, when Mum came into the kitchen and stared at the table in horror.

'Get down, you bad dog!' she shouted.

Oscar jumped down from the table.

'What on earth are you doing, Sam?' demanded Mum.

'I thought we better find out what Oscar likes to eat,' said Sam.

'He's a dog, he doesn't eat salad or lasagne!' said Mum. 'Dad's just been out to get some dog food.'

'But he doesn't like it,' protested Sam.

'Don't be ridiculous! How would you know?'

Sam's mouth hung open. He couldn't say Oscar had told him, so there was no way to answer.

'Has he licked *all* of this?' asked Mum, pointing to the food.

'Well no, not all,' said Sam. 'He only sniffed the yoghurt.'

Mum shook her head and started to dump everything into the bin.

'Sometimes I wonder what goes on in that head of yours, Sam,' she grumbled. 'These sausages are way past their sell-by date.'

Sam was about to protest but, too late, the sausages vanished into the bin. Oscar stared for a moment, then walked out of the kitchen in disgust.

Sam found him outside in the yard, which was littered with bike parts. Dad seemed to be taking the Grandem to pieces.

'You're giving up on it?' asked Sam.

'For now,' said Dad. 'I'm working on something else – a pop-up toaster that will land the toast on your plate.'

Sam thought this sounded fun, if possibly dangerous. He was keeping an eye on Oscar sniffing around the flowerbeds down the garden. It gave him an idea – if he couldn't show that Oscar was cheap to feed, at least he could prove that he wasn't messy. He hurried down the lawn. Luckily Dad was busy with his bikes and too far away to hear them talking.

'Couldn't you go now?' asked Sam, lowering his voice.

Oscar looked up. 'Go where?'

'No, I mean *go* in the flower beds,' said Sam.

'What for?' asked Oscar.

'It'll prove to my dad that you're not messy,' said Sam.

'I don't see how.'

'Because you're doing it in the garden,' explained Sam. 'Dad will be pleased, especially if he sees me clear it up.'

'I can't just go to order you know,' said Oscar, huffily.

Just then the front gate opened and Sam saw Mr Trusscot. Their neighbour often dropped by uninvited, generally to complain about something.

'Look out, it's old Fusspot,' muttered Sam.

'Ah, Mr Trusscot, always a pleasure to see you,' lied Dad, stepping over a wheel.

'Is that a dog?' sniffed Trusscot, as Sam and Oscar came over.

'Do you know, I think it might be,' replied

Dad. 'Nothing gets past you, does it, Mr Trusscot? But what can we do for you?'

Trusscot eyed Oscar rather warily. Dogs made him nervous.

'I have some news,' he said. 'Good news, in my opinion.'

'Really? Are you moving to Australia?' asked Dad.

Mr Trusscot ignored him. 'As you know, it's the Council's job to keep our streets clean,' he said. 'We've already done a splendid job stamping out litter but now we're going to tackle another problem. Dogs.'

'Dogs? What have they done?' asked Sam.

'What they've done is very much the point,' said Trusscot. 'I think we all know very well what dogs *do*.'

Sam and Dad looked at each other.

'I mean what they *do* in the parks, on the streets, in public places,' said Mr Trusscot, wrinkling his nose.

'Give us a clue,' grinned Dad.

Mr Trusscot sighed heavily. 'I am talking about *dog business*,' he said.

'Oh, *dog poo!*' cried Sam.

Mr Trusscot closed his eyes. 'This morning I counted twenty-four instances of *you-know-what* on the streets,' he said. 'It's an utter disgrace!'

'I agree,' said Dad. 'It stinks.'

Sam laughed, he couldn't help it.

Mr Trusscot rocked on his heels. He didn't like jokes, especially when he was deadly serious, which was all the time. He glanced at Oscar again, who was staring in a way that made him uncomfortable.

'Well, it's high time the Council took action,' he continued. 'If any dog is caught fouling the street the owner will have to pay a fine of two hundred pounds.'

'Two hundred pounds?' echoed Sam.

Dad frowned. 'Isn't that a bit steep?'

'Not at all,' said Mr Trusscot. 'And any dog that repeatedly does . . . what dogs do, will be locked up. From next week all dogs must be registered with the police, and that's just the beginning. We are going to set up dog-free zones, where no dogs are allowed. By the time I've finished, dog mess will be a thing of the past.'

Sam couldn't believe it. 'It's not the dogs' fault – you're treating them like criminals!' he protested.

'Dogs who foul the streets *are* criminals,'

declared Mr Trusscot, pompously.

Oscar raised his head and Trusscot flinched.

'Wouldn't it be better to find a solution?' asked Dad.

'I've just told you the solution,' snapped Trusscot. 'And I suggest you keep your dog on a lead.'

He jabbed a finger at Oscar, who'd evidently heard enough. He advanced growling.

'Keep back!' squawked the Councillor. 'SIT!'

Oscar did not sit. He kept on coming, driving their visitor back down the path.

'SHOO! Get away, you brute!' spluttered Trusscot, backing speedily towards the low front gate. Whether he thought it was open or not wasn't clear, but the next moment he clattered right into it. His legs folded and he performed a spectacular backwards flip, vanishing from sight.

A moment later his pink face surfaced over the gate. His bow tie was on sideways and he looked rather shaken.

'THAT DOG IS DANGEROUS!' he snarled. 'He should be LOCKED UP!' With that, he stood up and stormed off down the road, with as much dignity as he could muster.

Sam looked at his Dad, who seemed to be bent over in pain. It took a moment to realise he was doubled up with laughter.

'Oh dear – ha ha ha!' he wheezed. 'That's the funniest thing I've seen in years!'

But Sam was still annoyed at what Trusscot had said.

'Not all dogs are messy,' he said. 'I bet Oscar would never do that on the street.'

'All dogs do that on the street, Sam,' said Dad, still chuckling.

'Not all,' argued Sam. 'Dogs like Oscar are tidy. They make sure they go in the garden.'

He pointed to Oscar who had chosen this moment to do what dogs do. Unfortunately he'd chosen a spot right outside the back door step where someone was most likely to tread in it.

'Oh no, *not there!*' groaned Dad, throwing up his hands.

Chapter 5

Not at the Dinner Table

'Is he *always* like that?' asked Oscar when the two of them were alone.

'Who, Dad?' asked Sam.

'No, Mr Fussbottom.'

'Oh, him,' said Sam. 'I think it's because he runs the Council – he's very important and most of the time it makes him cross. Dad says he shouldn't be put in charge of a bag of jellybabies.'

'Well he certainly doesn't like dogs,' said Oscar.

Sam shook his head. 'You don't think he'd

really lock you up though?'

'Don't you believe it, I don't like the smell of him,' said Oscar. 'Anyway, what does he expect us to do? It's not as if there are dog toilets on every corner!'

Sam laughed. He wondered what a dog toilet would look like – perhaps it would be in the shape of a lamp post? When you thought about it, it wasn't such a bad idea.

Over supper they told Mum about Trusscot's visit and the Council's latest campaign. Mum thought that they were being a little bit hard on him.

'Well for once, he does have a point,' she said. 'You see a lot of dog mess on the streets and something should be done about it.'

'You can't go round locking dogs up! It's

cruel!' argued Sam. 'I mean pigeons don't go to jail and they plop on everything!'

Mum shot him a look. 'Well, it's the owners I blame,' she said. 'They should clear up after their dogs. Now can we *please* change the subject while we're eating?'

'He said he wants to set up dog-free zones!' Sam protested.

'Nutty as a fruitcake,' said Dad. 'I've said it before.'

Sam looked at him.

'Couldn't you do something?' he asked. 'You could invent something – like dog toilets, for instance.'

'Oh *please!*' groaned Mum.

Dad smiled. 'It's a nice idea, Sam,' he said. 'But you'd need hundreds of them.'

'And dogs wouldn't wait,' added Mum.

Sam had to admit this might be a problem.

'But there must be a better way,' he argued. 'There ought to be something that cleans up the mess.'

'It's called a pooper scoop,' sighed Mum. 'Now please can we talk about something else?'

But Dad was just getting interested.

'They are pretty hopeless, you have to admit,' he said. 'I mean who wants to get down on their knees and scoop muck into a plastic bag?'

Mum pushed away her dinner.

'Exactly,' said Sam. 'What you need is something that does the job for you. A muck cleaner or a Poopomatic or something.'

Dad stopped chewing and looked at Sam

'A Poopomatic,' he repeated. 'You know what, Sam, you might just be on to something there.'

'Really?' said Sam.

'Yes, yes, where's my notebook?' said Dad, getting up from the table.

Mum shook her head. 'Now look what you've done!' she sighed. 'It's like living in a mad house. It's bad enough having a shed full of bike parts, toasters and whatnot without you putting potty ideas into his head.'

Sam didn't think it was a potty idea at all, but Mr Trusscot's dog laws weren't their biggest problem right now. Time was running out to persuade his parents to let Oscar stay. Sam had tried to prove that dogs weren't messy or expensive but it had got them nowhere. He needed a new plan – and fortunately he'd come up with one. It was risky, however, and it needed Louie's help. That's why he'd asked his friend to drop round after supper. As soon as Louie arrived they took Oscar up to Sam's bedroom where they could talk in private.

'So what's this all about?' asked Louie. 'I can't stay long.'

'Well, you know my parents are always saying that dogs are a lot of work?' began Sam. 'What if we proved that Oscar is actually useful, that he can look after them?'

Louie frowned. 'How? By making them breakfast? He'd spill all the milk!'

Oscar snorted.

'No, I mean by protecting them,' said Sam. 'For instance, what if my mum was in some sort of danger and Oscar saved her?'

Louie's eyes lit up. 'Yes, that would work!' he said. 'Like if your house is on fire and you're all trapped inside. Then suddenly Oscar comes

flying in through the window like Superdog
and he drags you all to safety!'

'Kind of,' said Sam. 'Only we probably can't set fire to the house.'

'Oh no, I suppose not,' said Louie, sounding disappointed.

'But what if it was a robbery?' said Sam. 'Say a robber tried to steal my mum's shopping and it was Oscar who came to the rescue.'

'I like it,' said Louie. 'Except we don't know any robbers.'

'Well, obviously it couldn't be a *real* robber,' explained Sam. 'It'd have to be someone playing the part, like a friend of mine.'

Louie nodded slowly, and then his jaw dropped.

'No way! *I'm* not doing it!' he cried.

'It's only pretend,' said Sam. 'My mum goes shopping every Thursday. All you have to do is grab one of her bags and try to get away. When

Oscar catches you he'll be a hero and my mum will love him.'

'Yes, but I'll be the one she *murders!*' argued Louie.

'She won't even know it's you,' said Sam. 'Wear a mask or something to cover your face. Anyway, once Oscar's got the bag you can run off.'

Louie shook his head. 'Forget it. Ask someone else,' he said.

'There isn't anyone else!' sighed Sam. 'This is our best chance. You want us to keep Oscar, don't you?'

'Of course I do,' said Louie. He looked at Oscar who had been sitting very upright, paying close attention.

'Tell you what,' said Louie. 'If I do this, will you let me borrow Oscar sometimes and take him for a walk?'

Sam shrugged. 'Sure, as long as my parents let him stay.'

Louie's face broke into a grin. 'You're on then,' he said. 'And we'll need a code name for the plan. Let's call it "Operation Oscar."

Sam saw Louie out downstairs, agreeing to go over the final details of the plan the next day at school.

When he returned to his room Oscar was waiting behind the door.

'Well, what do you think?' said Sam. 'It's a great plan, isn't it?'

Oscar gave him a look. 'What do I know? I'm only a dog,' he said. 'People just borrow me whenever they feel like it.'

Chapter 6

Operation Oscar

On Wednesday afternoon events started to take over. Sam came home from school to find his Mum putting on her coat, ready to go to the shop.

'But you always go shopping on a Thursday,' he protested.

'Well, we're out of bread and milk so I'm going now,' replied Mum.

Oscar wandered into the kitchen. 'What now then?' his face seemed to say.

Sam needed to get in touch with Louie or they'd miss their chance altogether. He grabbed the phone in the hall and thumped upstairs with it. No one picked up so he gabbled a message, telling Louie to meet them at the shop as soon as possible. Fortunately, when he returned to the kitchen, Dad had come in from the shed with something to show them. It was a strange metallic box shaped like a wedge of cheese and sitting on twin caterpillar tracks. The top was dotted with a mass of dials and buttons. Sam thought it looked like something you might take on a mad expedition to the moon.

'What is *that*?' asked Mum.

'This? This is the answer to all our problems,' said Dad, proudly. 'Clear some space and I'll show you. We'll need something to act as the poop.'

'The *what*?' said Mum.

'Didn't I say? This is Sam's clever idea, the

Poopomatic,' explained Dad.

'What about a carrot?' asked Sam, taking one from the vegetable rack. Any delay was fine by him as it gave Louie more time to be ready.

'Perfect,' said Dad. 'Put it right there in the middle of the floor.'

Oscar trotted over and sniffed the carrot, perhaps hoping it was a sausage in disguise.

'Now let's say this carrot is the dog doo,' said Dad. 'Watch very carefully.'

He set the controls to 'ON'. Sam crouched down to watch. He was eager to see the invention work, partly because it was his idea. Oscar retired to a safe distance, not taking any chances.

The Poopomatic clicked and whirred into life, then beetled forward slowly on its caterpillar tracks. A red light flashed and it performed a sharp right turn, detecting the presence of the carrot posing as the dog doo. The machine stopped dead.

'Has it broken?' asked Sam.

Dad raised a finger to wait. The front of the machine flipped open and out came an arm shaped like a scooper. It picked up the carrot and swallowed it back into the machine. Sam was about to clap but the performance wasn't over yet. The red light flashed and the machine spun around. It beetled forward, this time making a beeline for Oscar. It chased him under the table, thudded into a chair leg and sat there buzzing and humming until Dad turned it off.

'Amazing!' cried Sam.

'Yes, it got a bit confused with Oscar at the

end but that's just a minor teething problem,' said Dad. 'You get the idea.'

'Very clever,' said Mum. 'But what's the point exactly?'

'Isn't it obvious? It's the answer,' grinned Dad.

'The answer to what?'

'The dog doo problem,' laughed Dad.

'I think it's genius!' said Sam.

Dad looked pleased but Mum still seemed unconvinced.

'Even if it works, who's going to buy it?' she asked.

'That's the beauty of it,' said Dad. 'Mr Trusscot!'

'You are joking?'

'Of course not,' said Dad. 'He's completely potty about dog mess on the streets – and the

Council are spending pots of money on it. Wait till he sees this, he'll be jumping for joy!'

Sam couldn't imagine Mr Trusscot jumping for anything unless he sat on a drawing pin. All the same, the Council did want to rid the streets of dog mess and anyone could see that the Poopomatic was the answer.

'Well, good luck with it,' said Mum. 'But right now we're out of bread and milk, so I'm going to the shop.'

'I'll come!' cried Sam, louder than he'd intended.

Mum looked at him in surprise. He'd never wanted to go shopping before.

'Oscar hasn't had a walk, so he can come along,' explained Sam.

He pulled on his trainers quickly, hoping that Louie was now on his way. Operation Oscar was on!

Chapter 7

Piggy Bike

The local shop in Little Bunting was called Greenway Stores. It sold bread, fruit, vegetables, sweets, bath plugs, ear plugs, phone plugs and just about anything you could think of. When they arrived, Sam suggested he should wait outside with Oscar, as dogs weren't allowed in the shop.

He paced around anxiously. Where on earth was Louie? He only lived five minutes away so what was taking him so long?

'Remind me, what are we doing here?'

Sam almost jumped. He still hadn't got used to Oscar speaking without warning. He checked that no one was about and crouched down beside him.

'I told you,' he whispered. 'When Mum comes out Louie's going to steal her shopping bag and run off with it.'

'And that's a good idea, is it?' asked Oscar.

'Yes!' said Sam. 'All you have to do is stop him getting away. Then Mum will think you're amazing, she'll tell Dad and they'll both let you stay.'

Oscar looked up at the grey sky. 'What could possibly go wrong?' he asked.

Just then a bike skidded into the shop forecourt, kicking up gravel. Louie had finally arrived.

'Where have you been?' complained Sam.

'I had to get ready,' explained Louie. 'You didn't say it was going to be today!'

He was dressed in jogging bottoms and a grey hoodie. He explained that this was part of his clever disguise, as it would help him blend into a crowd – not that there was a crowd.

'What about your face?' objected Sam. 'Mum will recognise you!'

Louie pulled something from his pocket and put it on. It was a rubber mask with the face of a pig.

'You can't wear that!' cried Sam.

'You said wear a mask, it's the only one I could find!' replied Louie

Sam shook his head. Trust Louie, the whole idea was *not* to attract attention, so he turned up disguised as a pig on a bike.

Sam glanced back at the shop. There wasn't time to argue – any minute now his mum might appear.

'Remember what we planned,' he said. 'Just grab the shopping bag and run for it.'

'Pedal for it,' Louie corrected him. 'I'm on my bike.'

'How can you carry a shopping bag on a bike?' demanded Sam.

'Over the handlebars,' replied Louie.

'Anyway, it's Oscar you should worry about. What if he doesn't chase me?'

They both looked at Oscar who was staring at a picture of a lost cat in the shop window.

'He will, don't worry, I've explained it to him,' said Sam.

Louie seemed puzzled, although it was hard to tell behind the face of a pig.

'She's coming!' hissed Sam. 'Hide!'

Louie wheeled his bike into the shadows out of sight. They were just in time as Mum came out of the shop carrying two bags.

'Sorry, I bought more than I planned,' she said, handing Sam one of them. It weighed a ton. He crossed over so that his mum would be on Louie's side.

'Okay?' she said.

'Yes, fine,' said Sam. His hands were sweating

the way they did when he was in trouble at school.

They set off towards the road. Where was Louie? He was taking forever! Sam stopped to scratch his head as a signal. He could hardly make it any more obvious.

'What's the matter?' asked Mum, turning round.

'Nothing. Just a bit of an itch,' said Sam.

At that moment they heard a screech of bike tyres and a mad-eyed pig came hurtling straight towards them at top speed.

Mum screamed and dropped the bag she was holding. They both had to leap aside or Louie would have run them down. As he whizzed by, he tried to grab the bag with one hand and missed it completely. He braked hard, jumped off his bike and ran back to get the shopping.

But Mum had recovered from her shock and seized one of the bag handles at the same time. She hung on and a tug of war began, sending oranges bouncing across the car park like ping pong balls.

'LET GO, YOU BIG PIG!' she shouted.

Sam watched them struggling. This was probably the worst robbery in history – a gang of guinea pigs could have done better!

At last Louie managed to yank the bag free. He leapt back on his bike and set off pedalling towards the road. The bag swung from the handlebars, making him wobble all over the place. Plainly in the mask he could hardly see a thing.

'Hey! Come back!' yelled Mum.

Sam awoke from his daze, remembering his part.

'OSCAR! AFTER HIM!' he cried.

Oscar, who had sat watching the whole thing, trotted after the bike. He didn't run, confident that Louie wasn't going to get far – and he was right. Seconds later, Louie narrowly missed a wall then collided with a man who'd suddenly appeared around the corner.

Sam groaned. Of all people it was their neighbour, Mr Trusscot. There was a crash as the bike went down and Louie flew off. The shopping spilled everywhere.

Sam and his Mum ran over. Mr Trusscot was sprawled on his back, squashed by the robber pig on top of him. All around, apples and tomatoes were scattered like confetti while eggs formed a gooey yellow puddle in the gutter.

Mr Trusscot pushed Louie off and lay there groaning. He had egg yolk on his jacket and a blob on his chin. Oscar trotted over and kindly licked it off. This seemed to bring him to his senses.

'UGH! GET OFF ME!' he spluttered, sitting up.

Seeing the robber, he reached out and tore the mask from his face.

'LOUIE!' gasped Mum.

Louie blinked at them, his face sweating.

'Oh hi, Mrs Shilling,' he said.

'But I don't understand!' said Mum. 'What's got into you? Why are you trying to steal my shopping?'

Louie rubbed his knee. 'Well,' he said, 'I think, um, maybe Sam better explain.'

Chapter 8

Facing Fusspot

Naturally the whole episode ended in a blazing row. Sam tried to explain that they hadn't meant any harm – it was only a *pretend* robbery – but no one was in the mood to listen. Mum was furious. She said it was it probably the stupidest thing Sam had ever done, which Sam thought wasn't fair because he'd done lots of other stupid things. He and Louie had to listen to a long lecture from Mr Trusscot who threatened to report them to the police. When they got home, Dad heard the whole story and he told Sam off too. Sam thought they might as well phone Miss Bramble since everyone else seemed to be taking a turn!

He wouldn't have minded if the plan had worked, but it had completely backfired. Instead of changing his parents' minds, he'd pushed them into a final decision. Mr Trusscot didn't help – he blamed Oscar for the accident and demanded that they pay for a new jacket. To cap it all, Sergeant Wilkins phoned that evening and Dad had to apologise for about half an hour. Afterwards he said Sam had proved he couldn't be trusted to look after a dog. Oscar only caused trouble and expense. He was going to the dog shelter on Sunday and that was the end of the matter.

On Thursday Sam decided it might be best to give his parents time to cool off. He hadn't given up all hope but he knew it would take a miracle to change their minds. Arriving home from school he found the Poopomatic in the back yard where his dad had been working on it. No one else seemed to be around except for Oscar. He was sitting on the back step, wearing Dad's woolly scarf round his neck.

'It's a pity,' said Sam, thinking out loud.

'Yes,' said Oscar. 'I like the colour but it keeps getting under my feet.'

'Not the scarf, I mean it's a pity Mr Trusscot hasn't seen this machine,' said Sam.

Oscar snorted. 'That big baby! He doesn't even like having his face licked!'

'I know,' said Sam. 'But if the Poopomatic actually works then the Council might buy it. And if they did, Mum and Dad could stop arguing about money. They might even think again about keeping you.'

Oscar chewed one end of the scarf. 'That's a lot of ifs,' he said.

'Yes, but it's a chance,' said Sam. 'Unless you've got a better idea?'

Oscar padded down from the steps. 'I'm still working on it,' he said. 'So you think we should show this to Mr Fussybum?'

'It's worth a try,' said Sam. 'He won't be at home now but I know where he works.'

Ten minutes later they arrived at the tall Council building with its impressive glass entrance. Sam had towed the Poopomatic all the way, attracting a few funny looks from passers-by. It was a bit of a struggle getting it through the revolving doors. The security guard at the desk looked up as they entered.

'Good afternoon,' he said, dryly. 'You have

an appointment, do you?'

'We're here to see Mr Trusscot, please,' said Sam who had practised this line on the way.

'I see.' The guard nodded at Oscar. 'I'm afraid dogs aren't allowed,' he said. 'He'll have to wait outside.'

'It's okay, Mr Trusscot knows him,' said Sam. 'He likes dogs.'

Oscar gave him a sideways look.

The guard thought for a moment, then leaned forward and lowered his voice.

'If anyone asks, I never saw him,' he said. 'Take the lift to the third floor.'

A minute later they stepped out into a bright waiting area with sofas and some tulips on a coffee table. The receptionist had red hair and glasses that made her eyes look enormous. She looked even more startled when she saw a dog

wearing a scarf and a boy pushing a strange metal box.

'Yes? Can I help you?' she asked.

'We're here to see Mr Trusscot,' said Sam.

'Is he expecting you?' asked the receptionist.

'Er well possibly.'

'Mr Trusscot doesn't see anyone without an appointment,' began the woman, 'so I'm afraid . . .' She broke off because Oscar was looking up at her with big soulful eyes and a bunch of tulips in his mouth.

'Good gracious, are those for me? said the receptionist, taking them. 'What an adorable dog!' She smiled at Sam. 'You better wait over there, he's in a meeting.'

Sam sunk into one of the sofas. 'Nice going,' he whispered to Oscar.

As the minutes ticked by, people passed

through and stared at them or smiled to themselves. Sam wondered if this was such a good idea, after all. Waiting to see Mr Trusscot was like sitting outside the head teacher's office. At last a door opened and the Councillor appeared, shaking hands with a tall woman.

'There's someone here to see you, Mr Trusscot,' said the receptionist.

Trusscot looked over. 'Oh. It's you,' he said, heavily. 'Dogs aren't allowed in here.'

'It won't take a minute,' said Sam, standing up. 'We just want to show you something.'

Trusscot smiled at the woman. 'My neighbour's son,' he explained as if children were always popping into see him. He beckoned Sam to follow.

'I can spare you three minutes,' he said. 'And for goodness' sake don't touch anything.'

Mr Trusscot's office smelled of leather and furniture polish. He had a large gold-framed portrait of himself on the wall. Oscar seemed more interested in the plate of cakes on the desk. Trusscot sat down and stared at the machine with its buttons, knobs and dials.

'What in heaven's name is *that*?' he asked.

'My dad made it,' said Sam proudly.

'Of course he did,' sneered Mr Trusscot. 'But what's it doing here?'

'That's what we want to show you,' explained Sam. 'Dad says it's the answer to your problem.'

'I don't have a problem,' said Mr Trusscot.

'You know, the problem you were talking about the other day,' said Sam. 'All the dog doo dah on the streets.'

Trusscot waved this away. 'As I explained, the Council's dealing with that. We don't need any help from you or your Dad's electronic dustbin.'

'It's called the Poopomatic,' said Sam. 'I thought of the name – because it automatically cleans up poop.'

'Lord help us!' groaned Mr Trusscot, rolling his eyes. 'Look, young man, right now I have far more important things to worry about, things you couldn't begin to imagine.'

'Like what?' said Sam. He was good at imagining. On the desk was a piece of paper and if he leaned forward he could just read the heading, upside down.

'QUEEN'S VISIT TO WINKLESEA'

'The Queen?' Sam blurted out. 'Not the *actual* Queen?'

'What other queen would it be?' said Mr

Trusscot, snatching up the piece of paper.

'I suppose you'll find out soon enough. Her Royal Highness will be passing through on Saturday on her way to Winklesea.'

Winklesea was the big town just along the coast. Sam glanced out of the window as if the Queen might appear at any moment. He had to admit it was pretty amazing. Little Bunting had never had a royal visit – the closest they'd come was when Prince Charming from the Panto had switched on the Christmas lights.

'But that's fantastic!' cried Sam. 'And the Poopomatic's just what you need to clean up the streets!'

Mr Trusscot shook his head. 'If dog owners do as they're told there won't be a problem,' he said. 'Now your three minutes is up. Thank you for coming. Goodbye.'

He marched towards the door but found Oscar blocking his path. Trusscot hadn't forgotten his encounter with the garden gate. Sam seized his chance and grabbed the cake plate from the desk, choosing a pink iced bun.

'Just watch this, then we'll go,' he said.

He dropped the iced bun and bent to switch on the Poopomatic, hoping that Dad had got it working properly.

Mr Trusscot jumped back as the machine beetled forward, beeping and clicking. In no time at all it located the iced bun. The scooper arm came out, swallowing the cake whole into the machine. Then it stopped and a red light flashed on and off.

'Is that it?' demanded Mr Trusscot, bending over it.

Plainly it wasn't, because a flap suddenly

opened up. The iced bun shot out like a torpedo, hitting the Councillor full in the eye.

Sam looked horrified. Mr Trusscot removed his hand from his eye and blinked several times. He looked like he had a black eye – or at least

one decorated with pink icing. He pointed to
the door. 'OUT!' he thundered. 'GET OUT!
NOW!'

'But what about the Queen? And the dog
mess on the streets?' asked Sam.

'There won't be any,' snapped Trusscot. 'Because dogs are banned! All dogs must be kept off the streets, by order of the Council!'

Sam opened his mouth, but too late, the door had slammed in their faces.

Chapter 9

Where There's a Dog ...

When they got home Dad was waiting at the gate, wanting to know where on earth they'd been. He eventually got the truth out of Sam and couldn't believe his ears. They should never have taken the Poopomatic without permission, he said crossly, especially since it wasn't finished. Thanks to Sam, the chances of the Council ever buying the machine were now about one in a million. Sam didn't mention the iced bun disaster – he felt it wouldn't help matters. All in all, he thought, they'd done a pretty good job of making a mess of things. Dad was annoyed, Mum was still mad at them, the Poopomatic had failed and worst of all, time was running out for Oscar. No owner had come forward, so on Sunday he would be packed off to the dog shelter.

The next day the royal visit was front page news in the paper. Frantic preparations in the town soon gathered pace. No one knew the exact route Her Majesty would take or if she was arriving by car, royal coach or motorbike. Nevertheless, the news was enough to send everyone into a state of excitement. Nothing this dramatic had happened in the town since the day an ice-cream van crashed into the Post Office, smothering it in chocolate sauce.

Sam watched in amazement as Beach Road was rapidly transformed. Pavements were swept and litter banished from sight. The streets were hung with bright flags that flapped and twirled in the breeze. Even the town sign, 'Little Bunting Welcomes Careful Drivers', was changed to read 'Little Bunting Welcomes Her Royal Maj'.

(The sign-writer had run out of space.)

There were other less welcome changes too.

Signs grew up like weeds in public places saying 'WARNING: NO DOGS ALLOWED!' Dogs were banned from the beach, the high street and even the public park. Sam began to think that Trusscot secretly aimed to turn *the whole town* into a dog-free zone. There were a lot of complaints from owners and Sam noticed a lot of dogs staring miserably out of front room windows because they hadn't been out for their usual walk. Mr Trusscot, however, was far too busy to pay any attention. He was everywhere in the town, directing operations like a general.

After supper on Friday, Sam took Oscar out for what might be one of their last walks together. The beach was forbidden so they headed down Ferry Road. Oscar had other ideas however. Five minutes into the walk he turned off down a different road and then vanished from sight.

Sam eventually found him down an alleyway, sniffing around some dustbins surrounded by a sea of rubbish. Oscar raised his head and barked.

'Oscar, there's nothing here,' Sam called out. But then something surprising happened. Two dogs emerged from the rubbish – lean, hungry dogs that hadn't had a bath in months.

One was an old boxer and the other a little white Jack Russell who yapped and danced around. Oscar seemed to know them since they greeted him like an old friend.

'Got any food on you?' he asked.

Sam shook his head. 'Where do they come from?' he asked.

'Here, this is their home,' replied Oscar.

Sam took in the back alley piled with cardboard boxes, tins, paper, plastic and other rubbish.

'They can't live here!' he said.

'Not all dogs have a warm bed and a boy of their own,' said Oscar. 'Anyway, it's not so bad, there are plenty of scraps and they come and go as they please.'

'But wouldn't they be better off in the dog shelter?' asked Sam.

Oscar wrinkled his nose. 'They can't stand being cooped up,' he said. 'The shelter's all right – you're looked after and fed, but some dogs need their freedom.'

'You mean dogs like you?' said Sam.

Oscar held his gaze a long moment and then looked away.

'I'll be fine,' he said quietly. 'Don't worry about me.'

Sam watched him with the alley dogs and wondered how he knew them. Was it possible that once this alley had been Oscar's home too? Had he spent weeks sleeping behind bins and rooting through rubbish for scraps? Oscar had a collar but he'd never spoken a word about his last owner, whoever they were. Perhaps he'd been badly treated or even abandoned? Whatever the truth, Sam knew he couldn't let it happen again. He didn't want Oscar to live in a shelter or a filthy back alley. Somehow they *had* to find a way to make his parents change their minds.

Oscar was talking to his friends. The Jack Russell yapped excitedly while the boxer added occasional growls.

'They've all had enough,' Oscar reported. 'Even the dogs who have owners. It's all these signs going up around town. Where are dogs supposed to go?'

Sam nodded. 'It's not fair,' he agreed. 'You can't suddenly ban dogs from the beach and the park. Why can't they ignore the signs?'

Oscar sniffed. 'You heard Trusspot, they'll lock us up.'

'They wouldn't!' said Sam.

'Don't you believe it, this is war,' said Oscar.

'No, Mr Trusscot has to be stopped before this goes any further.'

'Yes, but how?' asked Sam.

Oscar trotted in and out of the piles of rubbish, deep in thought.

'So the Queen's coming tomorrow?' he said. 'I suppose she's quite important.'

Sam laughed. 'Are you kidding? She's the *Queen*! She's got servants and palaces.'

'And dogs?' asked Oscar.

'Yes, dogs too,' said Sam. 'Corgis, I think.'

'Humph,' grunted Oscar. 'Yappy little things!'

'But what's that got to do with it?' asked Sam, feeling they'd got off the point. However it was no use asking Oscar since he'd wandered off again to talk to his friends.

Oscar didn't offer another word of explanation until they were half way home.

Then he announced that he'd come up with a plan, a plan that only a dog would have thought of. Sam knew one thing for certain – Mr Trusscot wasn't going to like it. He wondered if it was even possible to carry it off. Oscar for his part, seemed quietly confident.

'You know what they say,' he told Sam. 'Where there's a dog there's a way.'

'Who says that?' asked Sam.

'I do,' replied Oscar and wagged his tail, very pleased with himself.

Chapter 10

A Royal Welcome

Back home, Sam found a letter from the Council on the doormat.

Sam stared at the letter in disbelief. As if dog-free zones weren't enough, now Trusscot wanted to prevent dogs going out at all!

'He can't do this!' he said, showing his parents the letter.

Mum sighed. 'I'm afraid it looks like he has.'

'That's Fusspot for you,' said Dad. 'The Queen's visit has gone to his head. He's barking mad!'

'A total mutt case,' agreed Mum, laughing.

Dear Little Bunting Resident,

Please note that *ALL DOGS* must be kept off the streets between the hours of 9 a.m. and 2 p.m. on Saturday when Her Majesty the Queen will be passing through.

Dogs who go out will run the risk of arrest.

We hope that in this way the town will be looking its best.

Gerald C. Truscott

Little Bunting Town Council

'It's not funny!' said Sam. 'Why shouldn't dogs be allowed to see the Queen?'

'I'm sure Oscar couldn't care less,' said Mum. 'It's only for a few hours. He'll just have to stay indoors till it's over.'

Sam felt this was an outrage. How would Mr Trusscot like it if *he* wasn't allowed out? But there was another reason that the letter worried him. If the Council got their way, Oscar's plan was shot to bits before they'd even started.

By nine o'clock on Saturday morning a crowd had gathered all along Beach Road. From his bedroom window, Sam could see two old ladies outside his house sitting on folding chairs. They'd brought packed lunches, umbrellas, a pair of binoculars and blankets to cover their knees.

'I'm just going to Louie's,' Sam called down.

'Now?' said Mum. 'I thought we were going to get a good place to see the Queen.'

'I know, but Louie might join us,' said Sam. 'It's okay, I'll be back before it starts.'

He hurried to the back door where Oscar sat waiting. The two of them slipped quietly out of the house before anyone saw them. Sam hoped they didn't run into Mr Trusscot or a policeman or they were in big trouble.

'Okay, where do we start?' he asked.

They began on Wigglesworth Road where the houses had back gates leading onto a lane. Oscar raised his head and his barks echoed off the rooftops. They waited a few seconds and a chorus of barking came back in reply. It sounded as if many of the dogs had been left in the garden rather than locked in the house.

Sam hoped owners were all down at Beach Road waiting for the Queen to arrive.

They hurried down the lane. At the first two houses they drew a blank, but at the third one Sam opened the back gate and a ball of fur flew out. A little Yorkshire terrier raced around their legs, yapping excitedly.

At number eight a tall Great Dane almost flattened Sam as he bounded out of the gate. The terrier and the bigger dog gave each other a good sniffing before going over to sniff Oscar. At number fourteen they could hear barking but no dog appeared when they opened the gate. Oscar slipped into the back garden while Sam hung back anxiously.

'They might be in. What if we get caught?' he whispered.

Oscar took no notice. He was looking round the patio.

'There's probably a key,' he said. 'Where do people leave them?'

'I don't know, under a bin,' answered Sam. 'But you can't just break into someone's house!'

'We're not breaking in, are we?' replied Oscar. 'And anyway it's for dogs everywhere.'

They finally found a key hidden under a flowerpot and Sam unlocked the back door. A big Alsatian came bundling out to join them and the sniffing started all over again.

In half an hour they'd collected a small army, including a poodle, a mop-haired sheep dog, a little Scottie and half a dozen others of assorted sizes. The boxer and the Jack Russell from the alley turned up to swell the ranks.

They all seemed to follow Oscar as if he was their commanding officer. Sam half expected them to fall into line and bark out their names. He looked at his watch. 9.45 – he needed to get going.

'Will this be enough?' he asked.

'Plenty,' said Oscar. 'You remember what to do?'

Sam nodded. His mind was racing as he ran back to call for Louie. He couldn't quite believe they were actually going through with this, but there was no other choice. Trusscot's war on dogs had to be stopped before it went any further. If everything went to plan Sam hoped he might even be able to save Oscar – but there was no counting on that.

Back on Beach Road, Sam found a large crowd stretching all along the street. His parents stood outside their house and he and Louie joined them. Sam didn't dare breathe a word about Oscar's daring plan. In any case, Louie would probably ask how a dog could explain a plan in the first place.

Many of the crowd had little Union Jack flags, which they'd been told to wave the minute the Queen's car came in sight. Polite cheering was permitted, Mr Trusscot had explained, but no singing or chanting like football hooligans. Metal barriers ran all along the street to keep people back and Beach Road was closed to traffic. Sam thought it must be brilliant to be the Queen – no one ever cheered or waved flags when *he* arrived anywhere! Climbing onto his garden wall, he peered over the heads of the crowd.

Mr Trusscot was checking his watch while pacing impatiently. He had planned this day in minute detail so nothing could possibly go wrong. On one of his patrols, he caught sight of Sam's family.

'Ah, Shilling, where's that dog of yours?' he

asked. 'Safe indoors I hope?'

'He's at home, don't worry,' replied Dad.

'Dogs like that are a menace, always growling at people,' grumbled Trusscot.

'It was only *you* he growled at,' said Mum. 'I can't think why.'

Sam looked surprised – his Mum was actually defending Oscar!

'So when are you expecting the Queen?' asked Dad.

Trusscot checked his watch again. 'She's four minutes late,' he said. 'I do hope nothing's gone wrong.'

It was Louie who first spotted the royal party. People turned to look as a line of gleaming black cars came into view.

'It's HER!' muttered Mr Trusscot. He straightened his bow tie. 'Make way people!

Let me through, I'm a Councillor!' he cried.

Three black cars were making a stately progress down Beach Road. Sam craned his neck in order to see better.

'Which one's the Queen?' he asked.

'The one wearing the crown,' answered Louie.

'I can't see her yet,' said Mum. 'She'll be waving, I expect.'

Sam had seen the Queen waving on TV – she didn't wave like ordinary people.

Mr Trusscot had joined the other councillors and VIPs in front of the barrier. He seemed to be practising his bow, just in case the Queen decided to knight him for services to clean pavements.

The crowd cheered loudly, waving their flags. Everyone's attention was fixed on the fleet of royal cars, so they didn't notice what was happening at the far end of the road. Sam spotted it though – a dog trotting out from one of the side streets. Even from this distance there was no mistaking Oscar and soon he was joined by a small army of dogs. They looked like a wild gang of outlaws riding into town for a final showdown.

Sam's mum gasped as she caught sight of them.

'Isn't that Oscar?' she cried. 'How did he get out?'

'I don't know, but it looks like he's brought every dog in town,' said Dad. 'Old Fusspot will go up the wall!'

Sam climbed down and tried to push his way to the barrier. Meanwhile Mr Trusscot had spotted the four-legged invasion.

'Great heavens!' he gasped. 'Where did they come from? Sergeant Wilkins, do something!'

'ME?' said the sergeant.

'Yes, you're the police! Arrest them!'

Sergeant Wilkins hesitated. It was all very well to say 'Arrest them', but how? There were a lot of dogs, a whole pack of them, and they looked like they meant business. Besides, he'd never been on a police dog training course.

The royal cars had slowed to a crawl, unsure whether the dogs were part of some strange welcoming party. The crowd's cheering died away as they waited to see what would happen next. The Queen's visit was certainly turning out to be exciting, though not in the way anyone was expecting.

Oscar kept trotting towards the procession with the other dogs at his heels. Sam could see the big Alsatian and the Great Dane at the front. Every now and again the Yorkshire terrier popped up to run ahead excitedly before a bark from Oscar brought him back. Only once did the army threaten to break ranks when a ginger cat hopped up onto a wall. The dogs skidded to a halt and every head turned to the left. The cat arched its back, hissed and then vanished from sight, leaving the dogs to move on. Twenty paces from the cars, Oscar suddenly stopped and sat down. One by one the other dogs joined him, forming a ragged line across the road.

Sam found his parents and Louie beside him at the barrier.

'Do something!' whispered Mum. 'This is terrible!'

'They're only sitting down,' said Sam.

'Yes, but why do they have to sit *there*?' asked Dad. 'They're blocking the road!'

For a minute or two there was a stalemate with neither the royal party nor the gang of dogs giving any ground. Louie nudged Sam.

'There, in the middle car!' he whispered. 'That's HER!'

Sam stared at the woman in the back, who was dressed in a smart, pale blue coat and hat. Even without her crown he knew it was the Queen. She leaned forward to speak to her driver, maybe asking why a pack of flea-bitten mongrels was blocking the road. It was a good question, and Sam was probably the only person who knew the answer.

Chapter 11

A Messy Business

Someone had to break the deadlock and it was Mr Trusscot who made the first move. As Leader of the Town Council, he felt the whole fiasco made him look a complete fool.

Calling to Sergeant Wilkins, he made a rush at the dogs, flapping his arms like a bald eagle trying to take off.

'YARGH! SHOO! SCRAM!' he yelled.

The sergeant joined in. He ran after Trusscot, waving his police cap and shouting, 'HI! YIP, YIP!' in a strange, high-pitched voice.

Oscar barked. Immediately the Great Dane and the Alsatian rose up and began to growl menacingly. Mr Trusscot put on the brakes. His courage deserted him and he fled back to the barrier, throwing himself over head first. Unfortunately he landed on one of the old ladies who walloped him with her sandwich box.

'Oh well done, Mr Trusscot!' chuckled Sam's dad. 'You showed them.'

'I didn't know you could run that fast,' said Mum.

The Councillor scrambled to his feet, rubbing his bald head.

'I don't see what's so funny,' he bristled. 'This is all your fault!'

'Ours?' said Dad.

'You and your blasted dog! Why don't *you* do

something?' snapped Trusscot.

Sam was keeping his eye on the cars. A tall, silver-haired man had just got out of the one in front. He looked like the Queen's Under Butler or more likely her Private Secretary.

'Who's in charge here?' he demanded.

'I am!' said Mr Trusscot, hastily climbing back over the barrier. 'Gerald Trusscot, Little Bunting Council.'

'Well look here, Trusspot, can't you remove these dogs?' demanded the Secretary. 'They're keeping Her Majesty waiting.'

Mr Trusscot twisted his hands together. 'I do apologise, we're doing our best,' he wheedled.

A buzz of excitement went up because someone else had got out. Dressed in her pale blue coat and hat, the Queen was unmistakeable. After her spilled three excited corgis, tugging on their leads. Sam could hardly believe it – the Queen was standing on his road, right outside his house! This was the moment he'd been waiting for – now everything depended on Her Majesty.

'Will someone kindly explain what is going on,' she said.

'I am *so sorry*, your Majesty, we are dealing with the problem,' said Trusscot, bowing repeatedly. 'Sergeant, what are you waiting for? Arrest those dogs.'

'*Arrest* them?' repeated the Queen. 'Whatever for?'

'Well, for blocking the road, your Majesty,' replied Trusscot. 'And anyway they shouldn't be here at all, this is a dog-free zone.'

The Queen stared at him. 'I beg your pardon?'

'A dog-free zone, your Majesty,' repeated Trusscot, sensing he might have said too much.

The Queen's Secretary was standing close to the barrier. Sam reached out and tugged at his sleeve. He handed him a letter from his pocket, whispering something.

The Secretary read the letter and passed it over to the Queen. It was the one the Council had sent out yesterday, signed by Mr Trusscot.

Her Majesty read it through and a frown

clouded her face.

'Is this your letter, Mr Trusscot?' she demanded.

'Well yes, your Majesty,' admitted Trusscot, going very red.

The Queen gave him a withering look. 'You mean, because of my visit, all dogs are forbidden to go out?'

'Er . . . yes,' said Trusscot, helplessly.

'BOO!' yelled someone in the crowd and others joined in. 'BOO! SHAME!'

Sam looked around. This was working better than they could have hoped. But they hadn't finished yet – the tricky part was to come. Oscar barked and the corgis immediately looked up. They broke free from the Lady in Waiting in charge of them and scurried over to join the line of dogs. A good deal of sniffing took place.

The Queen turned to the Council leader.

'So, Mr Trusscot, are you going to arrest my dogs too?' she demanded.

'No, of course not, your Majesty,' spluttered Trusscot. 'It's just that some dogs are a nuisance. They . . . well . . . they make a mess.'

'The Queen's dogs are trained,' snapped the Secretary. 'They know how to behave.'

But no sooner were the words out of his mouth than it happened – the part of Oscar's plan which Sam felt was a gamble. Oscar had plainly said something to the corgis because now they were squatting down in the road, with their little tails twitching.

'Oh Lord! No!' groaned the Secretary, turning away.

An awkward silence fell. The Queen did not look amused. For a moment it seemed the royal visit would forever be remembered as a rather smelly disaster. But Sam caught Oscar's eye – this was his big moment and he had to hold his nerve. Sam wriggled through the crowd and in no time was back with a strange metal box dotted with knobs and dials.

'Excuse me,' he called out. 'I think I can help.'

With a little help from Louie, he lifted the Poopomatic over the barrier and climbed over himself. Sam had hidden the invention behind the garden wall ready for this moment. He tried to ignore the look of panic in his dad's eyes.

'And what is *your* name?'

He turned to find the Queen looking right at him. Sam swallowed, his throat suddenly dry.

'I'm Sam, your Majestyness,' he stammered.

The Queen smiled at him. 'And this is your

dog is it, Sam?' she asked.

Oscar had appeared at his side.

'Yes, this is Oscar, your Majesty,' Sam replied.

Oscar wagged his tail and rubbed against the Queen's legs.

'I am *so sorry*, your highness!' groaned Mr Trusscot.

'It's perfectly all right, I am used to dogs,' said the Queen. She patted Oscar's neck and turned to Sam. 'So tell me, what is this machine of yours?'

'It's called the Poopomatic, your Majesty,' explained Sam. 'My dad invented it.'

'For heaven's sake, boy, the Queen isn't interested in your half-baked ideas!' hissed Trusscot.

But the Queen raised a hand to silence him.

'And what does it do exactly?' she asked.

'If your Majesty has a moment, I can show you,' said Sam.

He said a prayer under his breath as he switched on the machine. This is it – do or die, he thought.

The Poopomatic hummed into life. It trundled forward on its twin tracks as the crowd watched in hushed silence. Just short of the dog dirt, the machine stopped. The flap opened up and out came the scooper arm, picking up the poop and swallowing it from sight.

Sam could hardly bear to watch. If the Poopomatic spat it out like last time, everything would be ruined, including the Queen's nice blue coat. There was a loud click.

'Keep back, your Majesty!' cried Trusscot, seizing the Queen by the arm. But this proved a mistake. Suddenly a royal bodyguard leapt on top of him, wrestling him to the ground.

'UMMMFFF! HELP!' yelped Trusscot.

Meanwhile the Poopomatic carried on going quietly about its business. A nozzle shot up and sprayed the road with something that smelled like air freshener. The machine then whizzed round in small circles, drying the spot with hot air. When it had finished, nothing remained on the tarmac but a small damp patch.

A silence drew out. The Queen nodded and patted her gloved hands together. It dawned on Sam that she was clapping. Soon the crowd joined in and the applause grew louder until it echoed all down Beach Road.

'Astonishing,' said the Queen. 'You know

I've always hated those silly plastic bags they give you. This is so much better. And your father made it himself?'

'Yes, your Majesty, he's over there,' said Sam, pointing.

At the barrier Mr Shilling bowed, beaming with pride. Sam even caught sight of his mum giving a little curtsey.

'Splendid,' said the Queen. 'And tell me, has anyone taken up your idea? It sounds like they should.'

'Not yet,' admitted Sam. 'We did try the Council but Mr Trusscot wasn't interested. He doesn't like dogs.'

'So it would seem,' said the Queen. She glared at Mr Trusscot, who was back on his feet, looking a little winded.

'Dog-free zones, Mr Trusscot,' said the Queen.

'I trust we've heard the last of them – and all your other silly rules and regulations?'

'Yes, of course, your Majesty,' mumbled Trusscot, bowing low. Clearly he wished he could disappear down a hole.

The Queen walked back to her car, with Sam following.

'Thank you for your help,' she said, 'And I wish you every success with the . . . ah . . .'

'The Poopomatic, your Majesty,' said Sam.

'Quite so. Now, if someone can ask these dogs to move . . .'

She broke off because Oscar was already trotting back towards his friends. When he reached them they all stood up as if on a signal. They trooped out of the road and formed two lines as a doggy guard of honour for the Queen. She looked back at Sam and raised an eyebrow.

'That's a very remarkable dog you have there,' she said.

At long last the royal cars moved off, with the crowd cheering and the dogs all barking madly. Sam saw the corgis peering out of the back window and the Queen's hand waved a final time.

He breathed out and his knees went weak. 'Holy moly!' he said.

He could hardly believe what had just happened. He had actually stood there talking to *the Queen herself*. Against all the odds, Oscar's daring plan had worked. The royal party had stopped, the Poopomatic had performed perfectly and they'd even forced Mr Trusscot to abandon his crackpot campaign against dogs. Sam could hardly have wished for anything more – well, maybe one thing more. Oscar stood watching the cars disappear, looking sorry that it was all over. It had been a day to remember, thought Sam, but if his parents sent Oscar away, then nothing would ever be the same again.

Chapter 12

Humble Pie

Early on Sunday morning Sam's dad had hurried out to Greenway Stores. He returned as they were sitting down to breakfast with a dozen copies of the local paper. Oscar lay on the rug. Sam hadn't heard his parents mention the dog shelter, but then they hadn't mentioned Oscar at all. Perhaps in all the excitement they'd just forgotten, but Sam knew that was wishful thinking.

Dad spread the papers on the table.

'Take a look at this!' he said, excitedly.

The story had made the front page of a

special royal edition. There were four or five pictures of the visit, showing Her Majesty and cheering faces in the crowd. In one photo the Queen and Sam stood side-by-side watching the Poopomatic at work. (The you-know-what had been left out of the picture.) Dad read the words underneath.

'Local schoolboy, Sam Shilling, shows the Queen his dad's ingenious invention. The Council admitted that they'd pooh-poohed the idea.'

'"Ingenious"! What do you think of that then?' asked Dad, proudly.

'Amazing!' said Sam. 'And really it's all thanks to Oscar.'

'Oscar? What do you mean?' frowned Dad.

'Well, if it wasn't for him the Queen would never have stopped at all,' Sam pointed out. 'She'd have driven right on past to Winklesea.'

'Well, yes,' admitted Mum. 'But you're not seriously suggesting he planned it all?'

'Why not?' asked Sam.

'Sam, he's just a dog!' laughed Dad.

They all turned to look at Oscar lying on the rug. He closed his eyes and the smallest sigh escaped him.

'In any case, it doesn't really change anything,' said Mum.

'Doesn't it?' asked Sam, his heart sinking.

'No. It's great that you met the Queen and it's in the paper,' said Mum. 'But we still have piles of bills to pay. No one actually bought the Poopomatic.'

Oscar looked up. Right on cue the doorbell

chimed 'Ding Dong Merrily on High' (another
of Dad's little jokes.)

'Who's that on a Sunday morning?' asked
Mum.

It was Mr Trusscot, who for some reason was

looking unusually sheepish.

'Ah, sorry to interrupt, I was hoping I might catch you,' he said, coming into the kitchen. He hung around awkwardly, fiddling with his bow tie.

'Would you like some tea, Mr Trusscot?' asked Mum.

'No, no, I won't keep you,' he said. 'It's just something I wanted to discuss.'

'If it's the bikes in the yard I'm getting rid of them,' said Dad.

'It's not that,' said the Councillor. 'The fact is . . . well, the Council have asked me to take up your offer.'

'What offer?' said Dad.

'To buy your contraption . . . invention,' said Mr Trusscot.

Sam looked at Oscar whose ears were

suddenly on alert.

'Really?' said Dad. 'You mean the same invention you called a half-baked idea?'

Mr Trusscot's cheeks burned. 'I may have been a little hasty,' he said. 'But never let it be said that the Council are, well, you know . . .'

'A bit dim?' suggested Sam.

Dad folded his arms. 'Well I don't know. The fact is there's been quite a bit of interest in my invention,' he said.

Mum shot him a warning look.

'How many did you want, Mr Trusscot?' she asked.

'Six,' replied Trusscot. 'At least to start with, possibly more if it proves successful. And as long as we can agree on a sensible price.'

Mum made a swift calculation. 'Two hundred pounds. Each,' she said.

Mr Trusscot made a strangled noise in his throat, but it was clear that he was under orders to reach an agreement.

'Very well, I will inform the Council that we have a deal,' he said.

When she'd seen Trusscot to the door, Mum returned, unable to stop smiling.

'Two hundred pounds *each*?' said Sam. 'That's . . . how much is that?'

'Enough,' answered Mum. 'Enough to pay off all our bills with some to spare. And then who knows, this could be just the beginning.'

'So business *is* picking up!' said Sam.

'Of course it is,' laughed Mum. 'He's a very successful inventor, your dad, with royal approval no less.'

They all laughed and Mum gave Dad a kiss while Sam covered his eyes.

'Wait,' he said, 'but you haven't said anything about Oscar. Does this mean we can keep him?'

Dad put his arm around Mum and they both smiled.

'Of course we're keeping him,' he said. 'It's Oscar we have to thank for changing our luck – and, anyway, he's part of the family now.'

Sam went over and knelt beside Oscar, hugging him round the neck.

'You're staying!' he whispered.

'I should think so too,' replied Oscar softly.

Dad looked up. 'What was that?'

'Nothing!' said Sam, quickly. 'I was just talking to Oscar.'

Look out for Oscar and Sam's next extraordinary adventure . . .

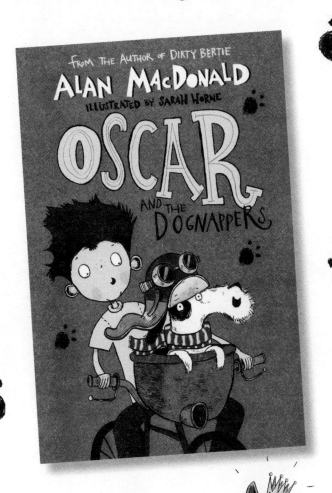

FROM THE AUTHOR OF DIRTY BERTIE

ALAN MacDONALD

ILLUSTRATED BY SARAH HORNE

OSCAR

AND THE DOGNAPPERS